STONE ARCH BOOKS
a capstone imprint

Published by Stone Arch Books in 2017
A Capstone Imprint
1710 Roe Crest Drive
North Mankato, Minnesota 56003
www.mycapstone.com

STAR38622

Cataloging-in-Publication Data is available
at the Library of Congress website.
ISBN: 978-1-4965-5347-8 (library binding)
ISBN: 978-1-4965-5356-0 (paperback)
ISBN: 978-1-4965-5363-8 (eBook PDF)

Summary: Harley Quinn has the blues. The Joker and
Poison Ivy have been nabbed by the Dynamic Duo.
What's a super-villain to do? Capture the Boy Wonder to
force the Dark Knight to set her friends free, of course!
Can Batman and Robin escape Harley's crazy creeper
caper? Or will they be forced to free two of Gotham
City's most notorious villains?

Editor: Christopher Harbo
Designer: Hilary Wacholz

Printed and bound in the USA.
072017   010584R

BATMAN & ROBIN ADVENTURES

HARLEY QUINN'S
CRAZY CREEPER CAPER

BY LOUISE SIMONSON

ILLUSTRATED BY
LUCIANO VECCHIO

BATMAN CREATED BY BOB KANE
WITH BILL FINGER

TABLE OF CONTENTS

CHAPTER 1

AMAZING PLAN A

Harley Quinn sat cross-legged atop a large, slightly damaged jack-in-the-box. It was just one of many strange artifacts in the storage room of the Joker's secret lair. Other pieces of equipment created by the brilliant criminal mastermind and inventor loomed around her. They stood as monuments to his evil genius.

Harley stared at a picture of the Joker and sighed. Crackers, one of her pet hyenas, laid a head on her knee and whined.

"I know, baby," Harley said, stroking his golden fur. "Things just aren't the same with Mr. J locked up in Arkham Asylum."

Harley sniffled. Then — *PLOP!* A tear fell onto the photo.

"It's Batman's fault! Batman *and* Robin's — for capturing my Puddin' and locking him up," she said. "Destroying our perfect partnership! Just 'cause he broke into a musty old museum and painted his beautiful smile on all the stodgy old masterpieces! It isn't fair!"

Crackers licked a tear from Harley's cheek, but Giggles, her other hyena, growled. He picked up his Batman chew toy. Then he shook it until it ripped and wads of stuffing spilled out onto the floor. Giggles dropped the shredded figure in Harley's lap and growled.

"You're right, Giggles!" Harley cooed, scratching him behind his ears. "Mr. J wouldn't want me sitting around feeling sorry for myself!"

Harley backflipped off the Joker's giant jack-in-the-box, landed, and threw back her shoulders bravely. "My Puddin' would want me to act! He'd want me to free him! He'd want me to get revenge! And that's exactly what I'm going to do!"

Both hyenas laughed with maniacal encouragement.

"You think I should talk to Poison Ivy?" Harley said as she reached for her phone. "I agree! Red's my best friend, and she's always up for some fun. I just know she'll want to help!"

***

Robin tugged at the ropes that bound his wrists behind his back. The cords were tight, but he could move his fingers. He ran his fingertips over the knot until he could identify it, as Batman had taught him.

"A surgeon's knot," the Boy Wonder announced.

"Good," Batman said, glancing up from the bank of computers he was studying. "You know what you're up against. Now all you have to do is free yourself."

Robin glanced around the Batcave. There were no sharp objects nearby he could use to cut the rope. He'd have to untie it, but this knot was difficult.

"We just captured the Joker," Robin grumbled, tugging at the cords. "I thought we could have some downtime. I want to play my new *Veggie Wars* video game."

Batman smiled over at Robin. "The sooner you free yourself, the sooner you'll be frying potatoes," he said. "Practicing your skills could save your life."

"I guess." Robin sighed as he pulled at another cord. "Other kids have normal homework. Sheesh!" But, already, he could feel the knot loosening.

Then, with a final tug, the ropes fell away. Robin leaped to his feet. "Victory!" he shouted. "Hello, video game!"

CLOMP! CLOMP! CLOMP! The Boy Wonder dashed up the stairs that led from the Batcave into the mansion above. He nearly crashed into their butler, Alfred, who was coming down.

"Good evening, Master Tim," Alfred said. He called down to Batman, "The Bat-Signal is shining over Gotham City."

"Ah, man!" Robin groaned.

"Apparently Poison Ivy is holding a property developer prisoner," the butler continued. "She appears to be helping a group of gardeners. They are protesting the developer's plan to put a building in an empty lot they use for a community garden."

"I have it, Alfred. Thanks," Batman said, looking up from his computer.

Robin glared down into the Batcave. One of the computer screens showed a green light blinking on a Gotham City map. Another screen showed a scene of confusion near a community garden. Batman was pulling on his bat-eared cowl. Robin sighed and trudged back down the steps.

"Don't wait up, Alfred. We may be a while," Batman said as he slid behind the wheel of the Batmobile.

Robin leaped in beside him. As they roared from the Batcave, Robin grumbled, "Good-bye, video game!"

***

The Batmobile pulled into a shadowed alley between a pair of old apartment buildings. Across the street, flashing lights from cop cars lit a row of police officers holding large plastic containers. An angry crowd blocking the sidewalk chanted, "Save our garden!" The police and the protesters were so intent on arguing, no one noticed the Batmobile arrive.

"Why are those people mad at the cops?" Robin asked as they leaped from the car. He gaped at the plants rising high and wild behind the protesters. "Shouldn't they be mad at Poison Ivy? There's no way they planted those monsters."

Robin was right. The garden was a wilderness of massive plants bearing vicious-looking flowers, threatening fruit trees, and hideous vegetables. Some plants were sprouting massive tentacles.

"That was a garbage-strewn empty lot until those people turned it into a garden. Now the police have been ordered to remove them," Batman said. They crossed the street, keeping to the shadows. "This isn't the cops' fault, but the police make a handy target. We need to end this situation before someone gets hurt."

Batman fired his grapnel toward the roof of a nearby apartment building. The hook caught on a ledge and drew him upward. Robin followed right behind him, flying up into the air. He landed beside Batman on a fire escape landing.

Below, the crowd's anger upset the plants. A monster tomato plant swayed like a baseball pitcher. Several giant red fruits flew from its stem, over the heads of the crowd.

PLOP! SPLAT! SQUISH! They splattered against the windshields of the cop cars.

"It'll take ages to scrape that off," growled a cop, hefting his container of weed killer and stepping forward. "This means war!"

"You can't use weed killer here," a protester shouted, trying to block the police. "Poison Ivy may be a criminal to you, but she's trying to help us! And that weed killer could poison her too!"

"Wrong," Batman murmured as he scanned the overgrown garden. "She's immune to all toxins, but the police aren't. Unless they're careful, they could poison themselves."

The Dark Knight took in the garden layout. "The plant beds form a maze."

"And there's Poison Ivy! Right at the center!" Robin said. "What's that thing she's waving in front of her captive?"

Batman studied the scene below. "It looks like she's trying to get him to sign a deed. Come on!"

As Batman and Robin swung down toward the center of the maze, Poison Ivy spotted them. She grinned.

"Harley Quinn!" she shouted. "Look who finally showed up!"

Poison Ivy looked around, like she expected her friend to whirl into the clearing like a small tornado. But nothing happened.

Ivy rolled her eyes. "Typical," she murmured. "And this was all her idea!"

CHAPTER 2

BRILLIANT PLAN B

Harley stood on a rooftop, her giant mallet slung over her shoulder, staring at the lights of Gotham City. At first it had been interesting, watching her pal Red transform that little garden into a monster maze. And then the cops had arrived. And the protesters had showed up.

Monster plants! A noisy mob! Angry cops! What a hassle! Harley turned her back on the chaos and glared toward Arkham Asylum.

Harley didn't care if that stupid developer signed over the garden to Ivy. All she cared about was getting revenge on Batman and Robin! It felt like she'd waited hours for them to show up.

The noise below seemed to fade to a dull rumble as Harley rested her chin in her hand and got lost in her memories. Her first meeting with the Joker when she had been his psychiatrist at Arkham Asylum. The time she popped out of a cake to take the police by surprise. The crazy capers she took part in to help her Puddin' achieve his mad, brilliant dreams.

"Good times." Harley sighed. If only she had been at the museum when Batman captured Mr. J. She just knew she could have saved him, and he'd have smiled and said —

"Harley Quinn!"

Harley blinked.

That wasn't Mr. J's melodious voice. That sounded like Red! And she sounded mad.

What?! Why? Oh! With a sinking feeling, Harley suddenly remembered why she was there. Her friend had been using her garden to lure Batman and Robin. They must have gotten here — and Harley had missed them!

In a near panic, Harley snatched up her massive mallet and leaped to her feet. She bounded across the roof, flipped onto the fire escape, and searched the garden below.

Batman and Robin were chasing Poison Ivy as she dodged through the maze of monstrous plants. A huge flower snapped at Batman, but he threw a Batarang, knocking it back.

KLONK!

A pumpkin plant shot a tentacle root toward Robin's foot, but he leaped over it. They were catching up to Harley's best friend, and Harley had done nothing to stop them!

She swung down to the bottom landing of the fire escape and cartwheeled onto the center of a giant sunflower. The air in the garden was thick with seeds and spores fired by the monster plants, but the Dynamic Duo kept on dashing after Red.

Harley was glad Red had made her immune to any toxins her plants might release. That was one thing she didn't have to worry about. She only had to save her friend. And she was almost too late!

SHWIP! SHWIP! SHWIP! Batman whirled bolos overhead. The heavy balls at the ends of the ropes flew blindingly fast. Then he threw them.

The bolos sailed toward Poison Ivy and twined around her, winding tighter and tighter until Ivy couldn't move. Batman began to run toward her.

Harley had one chance to save Poison Ivy. Balancing on the giant blossom, she pulled a pellet of knockout gas from her belt and tossed it at Batman.

The pellet struck the Dark Knight on the shoulder.

HISSSSSSS! The gas began to escape and cloud the air.

Yes! Harley thought. *I've saved her.*

Then Batman and Robin turned to look at Harley. She realized they were wearing clear plastic rebreather masks that blocked the gas. The seeds, spores, and even the knockout gas would have no effect on them.

Batman took Poison Ivy prisoner while Robin raced after Harley. The Boy Wonder climbed the stem of the giant squash plant, trying to reach her, but a vine grabbed his ankle and dragged him to the ground. *THUD!*

Robin scowled, trying to untangle himself, as Harley flipped and cartwheeled across the tops of the towering plants to freedom.

***

Harley watched from a rooftop as Batman carried Poison Ivy out of the garden. Robin followed with the rescued developer. The crowd muttered angrily.

As the police put Poison Ivy into the police van, she called out to the protesters. "Take care of my plants, and they'll produce enough fruits and vegetables to feed your entire neighborhood!"

"Except for the part where they attack anyone who tries to pick them," Robin said, rolling his eyes.

As the van door began to close, Poison Ivy looked up at the rooftop where Harley was hiding. "Take care of my plants!" she shouted.

The property developer turned to face the angry crowd. "Look, I didn't realize how much this garden meant to you," he said with a nervous smile. "Batman explained it to me, and he had an idea I think will work for all of us. What if we move your garden to the roof of the building I'm going to build? Your plants will get even more sunlight and fresh air on the rooftop."

The people murmured to each other. They sounded less angry now, like they thought Batman's idea might be a good one.

Harley watched as the police van rolled down the street, carrying Poison Ivy to Arkham Asylum. The protesters thanked Batman and returned to their apartments. Finally Batman and Robin roared away in the Batmobile.

While Harley watched and waited, she had time to think. She wasn't happy with the way she'd acted.

"Red was awesome!" Harley sniffed. "She helped those people, and she tried to help me. And now she's going to be stuck in Arkham Asylum, and it's all my fault. If only I'd been paying attention." She wiped away a tear. "I feel like such a screw-up!"

She knew that when Red had called out, "Take care of my plants," she was really talking to Harley. She would have to feed and water her best friend's plants every day.

Since she got Red captured, it was the least she could do.

***

Harley entered Poison Ivy's secret lab and greenhouse with its damp tropical heat and rows of giant mutant plants.

During the day, the room was brightly lit by skylights, but at night rows of plant lights, high on the ceiling, came on automatically. Harley realized that Red's plants had grown even bigger and stranger than the last time she had been there.

"Awesome!" Harley said.

She filled a large watering can with water and plant food just the way Red had shown her. Then she wandered up one aisle and down another. She watered the plants and talked to them as her best friend always did.

"Well look at you!" she told a looming flower that looked like a giant Venus flytrap. She read the sign. "Fangus creepola! Is that your name? You sure are a pretty one!"

CHOMP! It snapped at her playfully as she walked past.

"You've gotten so big!" Harley told a tentacula plant as she slipped under its reaching tentacles. "No hugs now. I'm busy."

As she walked up and down the aisles, she explained to the plants why she was there and what had happened to Poison Ivy.

In the far corner of the room, she discovered a plant she had never seen before. The bushy little plant had pointy leaves and bright red berries. Like a holly plant, she realized. But bigger. As she approached, it rose up on its roots and reached gracefully toward her.

It was beautiful, but she discovered that its pointed leaves were razor sharp and left scratches where they touched her.

"Wow!" Harley said admiringly. "Baby, you got claws!"

Then she read the sign attached to its bright red pot: The Harley Holly! Prickly, poisonous, precious.

"You're named for me?" Harley squealed. "Red created this beautiful, deadly plant and named it for me!"

And suddenly, Harley felt sadder and lonelier than she had before. "Now Red is gone, and I have no one. Not my Puddin'! Not my BFF!" she wailed. "And it's all my fault! I'm such a loser!"

The tentacula plant wrapped her in its massive tentacles. It hugged her.

"It's trying to comfort me," she told herself. Only, it was squeezing her now. Much too tightly. She was having trouble breathing.

The fangus creepola leaned toward her. Its petal jaws opened wide.

"Wait." Harley pulled away hastily, then backflipped away from the plants. Maybe they weren't playful and loving. Maybe they were mad at her. Except . . .

"Maybe . . . maybe I'm not a loser," Harley said to the plants. Poison Ivy was always telling her to stop and think. That's just what she needed to do now. "Red is an awesomely cool person, right? And an awesomely cool person would never have a best friend who's a loser! She asked me to take care of all of you! And no one would ask a loser to water her plants!"

The plants moved restlessly. They were still mad.

Keep talking, Harley told herself. *I know Red is still gone, and that's definitely somebody's fault. Since it's not mine, whose is it?*

Once Harley looked at it properly, the answer was obvious. It was the people who captured Red, the same people who captured the Joker.

"It's Batman's fault! And Robin's! So listen up!" Harley told the plants. "We're done with being mad at me. From now on, we're all going to be mad at Batman!"

Harley was going to come up with a brilliant plan that would make *him* feel like a loser. And she was going to make him give her friends back.

All Harley had to do now was figure out how to do it!

***

Several hours later, Harley slipped quietly into the Joker's secret lair. Despite the moonlight shining through the skylight, it seemed as dark as Poison Ivy's lab had been bright.

Harley looked warily at the creepy dark shapes that rose around her. Discarded equipment, half-finished gadgets, the giant broken jack-in-the-box — all brilliant machineries of the Joker's clever illusions.

I'll think of something, Harley thought. *A clever plan that will make Poison Ivy and Mr. J proud!*

Out of the corner of her eye, Harley saw movement. She whirled.

A two-headed monster loomed over Harley, wide jaws opened and slobbering.

It whined.

And Harley realized that what she saw wasn't a scary, two-headed monster at all. It was the twisted reflection of her pet hyenas in one of the Joker's many fun house mirrors.

Harley flung her arms around her pets and hugged them tight.

"Thank you, sweet babies! You just gave me a brilliant idea!"

SLURP! SLURP! The hyenas licked Harley's face happily.

"I'm going to use those mirrors to kidnap that annoying Boy Wonder," Harley said. "I'm going to show Batman how it feels to lose someone he cares about. And I'll make Batman set Poison Ivy and Mr. J free!"

CHAPTER 3

TRIUMPHANT TRICKS

Captain Speckleye rolled from behind his spaceship. His multiple eyes searched the hangar for the caterpillar that was his enemy. It was kill or be killed in *Veggie Wars*.

Speckleye raised a blaster in one of his tentacles, but Tim was ready for him.

"Fry!" Tim shouted as he fired his fryer at the many-eyed monster. "Fry, potato slime! Fry!" He punched the game controls like a maniac.

POW! POW! POW!

On the TV screen, Captain Speckleye exploded into French fries. *Yes!*

A door in the hangar slid open, one Tim knew led to the level boss —

"Excuse me, Master Tim," Alfred said. "You need to see something on the news."

The butler picked up the TV controls and *CLICK!* He switched the screen from Tim's video game to a news bulletin.

Tim groaned. "What now?"

The news showed an image of Harley Quinn using neon green spray paint to write "HARLEY <3 MR. J" across the front of a tall stone building. The image panned past Harley to a gargoyle that looked like a hippopotamus. It was perched on the roof, above a massive column. The hippo's stone face wore a red spray-painted Joker grin.

"This video, shot by a passerby, shows Harley Quinn tagging the Gotham Museum of Natural History," the news anchor said. "She has defaced the main entrance and several animal gargoyles on the building. The police are on their way, but this time not even they may be able to stop her."

"Good grief, Alfred! What is going on with Gotham City's super-villains?" Tim grumbled.

"Perhaps now that the Joker is in Arkham, Harley Quinn is trying to take his place," Alfred said. "Or she may have another goal. Whatever her motive, Master Bruce requests that you join him in the Batcave."

Moments later, Tim clattered down the steps into the Batcave. Batman waited near his bank of computers, studying the screen that was showing Harley's antics. Another screen displayed a blueprint of the museum.

Tim snatched up his Robin outfit. "First the Joker, then Poison Ivy, and now Harley Quinn! What is this — Crazy Super-Villains Act Out Week?" he grumbled as he changed into his costume.

"Come on!" Batman strode toward the Batmobile. "We have to hurry!"

Tim dashed after him. "Just tell me why," he muttered. "Why can't I play a simple video game in peace?"

VROOOOOM!

As the Batmobile roared from the Batcave, raindrops spattered against its windshield.

"And now it's raining," Robin groaned.

Sheets of rain hammered against the roof of the Batmobile as Batman steered it over the O'Neil Bridge and into downtown Gotham City.

"At least there's not much traffic," Robin said. "It's way past rush hour."

Finally, through the downpour, they spotted the museum. The massive building had been enlarged several times in a jumble of styles over the last century. Its famous stone gargoyles, carved in the shapes of animals, looked down from the front edge of the roof.

The Batmobile rumbled past cop cars parked in front of the museum. Police spotlights swept across the main entrance. Through the rain, Harley's neon green words gleamed bright and clear: HARLEY <3 MR J.

The Batmobile turned a corner onto a quiet side street. Halfway down the block, it pulled into an alley across from the museum.

"We're going to go after her?" Robin asked. "Up the back of the building?"

Batman nodded. "The rear of the main wing has two towers covered with thick vines." He slid from his seat. "We won't even have to use our grapnels to reach the roof."

"Harley probably went up that way too," Robin said as he climbed from the car. It was like stepping into a cold shower. "Are we sure Harley's still there?"

"Alfred says so," Batman said, tapping the communicator in his ear. "Apparently her attention is on the police and reporters at the front of the building. If we keep to the shadows, we should be able to surprise her."

"If we can even make it to the roof! The way it's raining, this is going to feel more like swimming than climbing," Robin grumbled. He glared at the cowl that covered Batman's head. "Next time, I want a waterproof uniform. With a hood."

Batman and Robin sloshed through puddles to the castle-like tower with its clinging vines. Batman tested them to make sure they would bear his weight. Then he started to scale the wall.

Robin climbed slowly, copying Batman's moves. Water beat his face and the vines were slippery. He placed his feet carefully.

Finally, Batman reached the roof and peered through a notch at the top of the tower. Robin pulled himself up beside him, squinting to see through the curtain of rain.

The roof was wide and more than a city block long. It was broken up by a jumble of odd shapes — walls of different heights, air conditioning equipment, vents, storage sheds, and even a water tower. The animal gargoyles edged the front of the building.

"There," Batman whispered.

Across the roof, Harley sat atop the back of a lion gargoyle. A police spotlight turned the raindrops around her into glittering diamonds as she leaned over. Then she swiped a can of spray paint back and forth across its face. *HISSSS! HISSSS!*

Robin knew the lion now wore a bright red Joker-like grin.

Harley rose gracefully, stood on the lion's back, and bowed to the police and reporters on the ground below. Then she flipped off the gargoyle and onto the roof.

"Show-off," Robin muttered.

While she was distracted, Batman and Robin pulled themselves up onto the roof. Then lightning flashed, bleaching the world to white. *BA-BOOOM!* Thunder roared like a cannon. And when they looked for Harley, she was gone.

"She's an acrobat, not a magician," Robin whispered. "She didn't just disappear. Do you think she saw us?"

Batman peered into the rainy darkness. "Impossible to tell," he said. "If so, there are lots of places up here for her to hide."

They looked around.

"That way," Robin whispered, pointing right. "I think I saw something move."

"I saw a flash on the left," Batman said. "It's impossible to see details in this rain. You check right. I'll go left. If you find her, shout."

Batman watched Robin disappear into the rain and darkness. Then he turned toward the flicker of light he thought he had seen — maybe a reflection or the gleam of a tiny penlight. Whatever it was, he thought it disappeared behind a storage shed.

Keeping to the shadows, Batman crept soundlessly from one dark shape to another. Finally, the shed was before him. He was halfway certain he'd find Harley Quinn crouching on the other side.

Batman slipped to the edge, then whirled around the corner, bolos in hand.

Harley was standing there, half hidden by the rain, and looking oddly warped. Behind her was — a giant flowering plant!

Batman hurled the bolos, expecting its rope to wrap around her as it had Poison Ivy. Instead — *WHACCKKK!* — it slammed into a hard surface that cracked beneath the force of the blow.

In that instant, toxic spray from several of the plant's huge blossoms hit Batman right in the face.

The pouring rain washed away some of the poison. It gave Batman time to realize that what he had seen was a distorted reflection of Harley in a mirror — one of the Joker's fun house mirrors! Then the nerve toxin paralyzed him. **THUNK!** He collapsed onto the roof, unconsciousness.

"One down! Easy-peasy!" Harley whispered. "Good plant! Now on to the Boy Wonder!"

***

Robin crept across the roof. He was alert and careful, searching with his eyes, listening with his ears for Harley. But so far he had found no trace of her.

As Batman had taught him, Robin tried to put himself into the mind of the villain. He tried to understand what she might do next.

Harley was on a mission, Robin realized, painting Joker grins on the gargoyles in a bizarre tribute to her beloved. All he had to do was move toward the front of the building and check them out, one by one, until he caught up with her.

She had already decorated the first gargoyle Robin checked. And the second. But the third — ?

There it was! That telltale flicker of movement! Robin leaped forward and saw . . . himself! It was a nightmare version, distorted in a fun house mirror. And Harley was behind him!

The Boy Wonder whirled, ready to fight.

Harley hit him with her mallet, knocking him backward. Robin slammed against something soft. He looked up . . . into the underside of a giant mushroom.

WHOOSH!

Before Robin could pull out his rebreather mask, a mist of toxic spores showered down on him.

One second later, the Boy Wonder was unconscious too.

***

Harley used a rope to lower Robin to the soggy grounds, then she climbed nimbly down the clinging vines after him. She lifted him over her shoulder, glad of the enhanced strength her pal Red had given her. Then, keeping to the shadows, Harley lugged Robin toward a clump of large bushes where she had hidden the Joker's car.

She popped the trunk and dropped Robin inside. "Sleep well, Boy Wonder," she whispered as she slammed down the lid.

Now that her plan had worked brilliantly, Harley felt better. She turned up the radio and sang loudly as she drove calmly toward Poison Ivy's secret greenhouse lab.

The rain finally stopped. It had lasted just long enough. All in all, it had been a perfect night for a kidnapping.

***

Robin struggled awake. His head hurt. He was standing upright and realized he wanted more than anything to lie down. But when he tried to move, he found it was impossible. Robin was tied in place, with his hands bound behind the pole at his back. He felt groggy and confused.

Wherever Robin was, it was hot and damp. And what was that awful smell? Like spoiled, rotting meat.

The Boy Wonder forced his eyes open and stared into the open maw of a large, green and purple monster with long, sharp teeth.

"Yow!" he cried. The monster jerked back.

Not a monster, Robin realized. Or not exactly. A gigantic Venus flytrap! That stink was the scent it used to lure its prey! And beyond it were other monstrous plants. Huge, ferocious ferns. Mushrooms as big as trees. Some plants had massive thorns. Others had twitching tentacles in place of leaves.

"So, you're awake," Harley said, cheerfully, as she popped out from behind a towering mushroom. "Welcome to Poison Ivy's secret laboratory and greenhouse!"

Harley was wearing an apron over her costume and carrying a huge watering can. As she skipped down the aisle toward Robin, she bent to water one plant, then another.

A prickly-looking holly bush followed at Harley's heels. It lurched along the ground on tentacle-roots, like a pet plant.

"Nice outfit," Robin croaked, trying to sound brave. "You know Batman is going to come after you?"

"Not if he wants to see *you* alive." Harley grinned at him as she carefully watered the giant Venus flytrap. "If Batman doesn't do what I tell him, I'm going to feed you to the fangus creepola. I call it Fang for short!" She stroked one of the flytrap's giant leaves.

As if Fang understood what Harley said, it leaned forward and nipped at Robin.

SNAP!

It could almost reach him. If he hadn't jerked back, it would have bitten off his nose.

CHAPTER 4

POISONOUS PAYBACK

Batman awoke, lying in a puddle, looking up at the moon. It was half covered by lingering clouds, but it was bright enough to show the old-fashioned water tower. So he knew he was on a roof. But what roof?

The Dark Knight felt dizzy and confused, but he needed to think.

He forced himself to sit upright — and stared into the face of a huge horned demon.

Something grabbed his neck and dragged him backwards. Another demon?

As Batman twisted away, he pulled a
Batarang from his Utility Belt and hurled
it over his shoulder at his unseen attacker.
THUNK!

The grip on Batman's neck loosened. He
rolled away and stumbled to his feet, ready
to face the demons.

But his attacker wasn't a demon. It was
a giant flowering rosebush with leaves
like writhing tentacles. Even now, one was
reaching for his ankle.

Batman stepped back and, as his head
began to clear, he could see there weren't any
demons. He had been staring at a twisted
version of himself in one of the Joker's fun
house mirrors.

And that plant? It had to be one of Poison
Ivy's monstrous creations.

Batman pulled the rebreather mask from his Utility Belt and clamped it over his nose. It snapped in place as a monstrous flower spat an odd mist at him.

Breathing the filtered air made it easier to think. *What is the last thing I remember?* Batman thought.

He and Robin had been on the roof, but they'd split up, each sure they knew where Harley had gone. *So where is Robin now?*

"Robin!" Batman called. He got no answer. Still feeling the effects of the toxic spray, he stumbled off in search of his partner.

Toward the front of the building, Batman found another of the Joker's fun house mirrors. And a giant mushroom. And, below the plant, moonlight glinted off strange, sparkling dust.

"Another toxin," Batman muttered.

Glad he had kept on the rebreather, the Dark Knight bent to study the spray of spores. In the middle of the spores was the faint outline of a fallen boy.

Robin had clearly been here. He had probably been surprised, as Batman had been, by the Joker's fun house mirror. And he had fallen victim to Poison Ivy's toxic mushroom spoors.

It was clear now that Harley's mad antics on the rooftop had been more than a simple show of her undying love for the Joker. They had been bait to lure Batman and Robin onto the roof.

Harley had set up the Joker's mirrors to trick them and Poison Ivy's plants to knock them unconscious. The storm had made it hard to see what was really happening.

It had been a carefully set trap, using weapons taken from the lairs of Poison Ivy and the Joker, their most recent captures. Harley had taken Robin, but she had left Batman behind. Where had she taken him? And why?

One thing was clear. Harley was sending a message.

Drag marks showed where Harley had pulled Robin's body to the edge of the roof. Rope shreds showed how she had lowered him. Broken leaves and vines marked where she had climbed down herself. Batman followed.

Harley's footsteps, sunk deep into the earth from carrying Robin, led to bushes where she had hidden a vehicle. Its tire tracks led to the street. And that's where Batman lost her.

Grimly, Batman slid into the Batmobile. At the very least, he knew what direction Harley had driven. But even though she thought she had been clever, Harley had also left a number of clues behind. Now it was up to him to understand them — to figure out where she had taken Robin.

It was long after midnight as the Batmobile roared down the deserted midtown streets. As it sped toward the O'Neil Bridge, its headlights revealed a message, scrawled across its footings in neon green paint:

Dear Batman,

Free the Joker and Poison Ivy from Arkham Asylum by dawn, or I'll feed Robin to a man-eating fangus creepola.

Sincerely,

Harley Quinn

Batman called Alfred and explained what had happened. "This message confirms my suspicion. Robin is being held near a monstrous man-eating plant. Which probably means Harley has taken him to Poison Ivy's secret lab."

Then he told Alfred his plan.

Alfred had known Bruce Wayne since he was a child, long before he became Batman. He was used to emergencies.

"I'll have the Batplane ready when you arrive," Alfred said calmly. "You'll have approximately four hours to find him."

***

Robin watched Harley watering several plants and talking to them. She glanced at him from time to time, making sure he noticed what a caring friend she was being.

But Robin knew Harley loved action. He was sure she would soon get bored.

Robin was right! Harley plopped down the watering can and vaulted onto the top of a giant mushroom.

"I miss the Joker and Red, and it's all your fault. Your fault and Batman's." Harley stood on her hands. "But don't worry! I told Batman to free the Joker and Poison Ivy."

"What makes you think he will?" Robin asked, playing for time. Harley had tied some excellent knots. He was having trouble getting them undone, but he had another option, if he could reach his Utility Belt.

"Because Batman would never let me feed you to a man-eating plant!" Harley chattered on. She did handstands and backbends to show off her gymnastic skills while she bragged about her own cleverness.

Harley didn't notice when Robin slid a finger to the side of his belt and flipped up a catch on one of its pockets. She didn't see him reach in for a wire that was coiled there. It had been coated with a chemical Batman had invented. When the wire was broken, the chemical would start to burn. Robin planned to set fire to the rope that bound his wrists. In a short time, he'd be free.

Fang, the Venus flytrap, had also noticed Harley was distracted. As Robin reached the wire, the plant stretched its stem toward him. It moved slowly, carefully, so Harley wouldn't notice. Its huge round head was drawing nearer to Robin's. Its jaws were opening.

Robin reached the wire. He grabbed it, stretched it tight, and **CRACK!** He snapped it in two. With a hiss, the wire ignited in a small, bright burst of flame.

Fang jerked back in horror. The flytrap's head slammed into the mushroom where Harley was balancing. First the mushroom, then the other plants pulled away in terror.

Harley noticed and flipped onto the floor in front of Robin. "Hey, what's that smell?" she snarled. "What's burning?"

Then she saw the flame that was beginning to eat through the thick ropes.

She snatched up the watering can and **SPLOOSH!** She dumped its contents over Robin's head, down his back, and over his hands. The flame went out.

So much for that trick, Robin thought. *I'll just have to free myself the old-fashioned way.*

Still, the experiment had been interesting. He hadn't realized the plants would be afraid of fire.

"Good try!" Harley snarled. "But there's no way you'll escape!"

"Doesn't matter," Robin growled. "Batman will be here soon anyway!"

"No way!" Harley scowled at him. "Batman doesn't have a clue where you are!"

***

Batman leaped from the Batmobile and helped Alfred load the final pieces of equipment into the Batplane. It was a flexible craft that could move like a jet or a helicopter.

"Are you sure this will work, sir?" the butler asked.

"Poison Ivy will have a large number of experimental plants in her lab," Batman said as he bolted an infrared scanner in place and threw a switch. The machine hummed to life.

"Those monsters are just too large and dangerous to keep out in the open or even in a normal greenhouse," Batman continued. "They'll be hidden away, probably within a special warehouse."

"And you think you can find it?" Alfred said anxiously.

"There'll be plant lights to keep her experiments alive and healthy, and they'll put out a lot of heat," Batman replied. "I'm going to find that heat signature, and when I do, I'll find Harley Quinn and Robin."

Alfred watched as the Batplane lifted from its launch pad and flew out of the Batcave.

"I hope you're right," Alfred murmured.

CHAPTER 5

DREADFUL DEFEAT

As Batman soared over Gotham City, he studied a map on the Batplane's computer screen. It showed the city in great detail. Tonight, his focus was the piers and buildings along the Gotham River shoreline.

"Highlight the buildings used as warehouses," he told the computer.

On the screen, buildings along the shoreline blinked yellow. "Selection complete," a computerized voice said.

The map showed a lot of warehouses. But Batman knew Poison Ivy would raise her plants under ideal conditions. Between the lights and the moisture, the warehouse he looked for would feel like a rainforest.

"Scan warehouses for unusual heat signatures. Temperatures between 82 to 90 degrees Fahrenheit," Batman said.

As the Batplane cruised over the shoreline, the instruments sounded a few soft pings. Batman checked the locations, but their temperatures weren't quite high enough to be Poison Ivy's lab.

Time was running out.

Batman flew further inland. Suddenly, loud pings alerted him. A warehouse, three blocks back from the shoreline, glowed like a beacon on his scanner. The building's temperature was 89 degrees.

Flying toward it, Batman saw the roof was dotted with glowing skylights. Inside the warehouse, bright lights were shining.

Batman dropped the plane lower and hovered. Moisture had collected on the glass. It was impossible to see inside. But he was sure he had found what he was seeking.

As the plane settled on the rooftop, its wheels made a soft *THUMP!* Hoping Harley hadn't noticed, Batman leaped to the ground.

***

Harley Quinn looked up as something thumped on the roof. "What was that?" she muttered.

Robin grinned at her. "Three guesses!" He was in good spirits. He had been working at the ropes for the last hour and finally they were beginning to come loose.

Harley scowled at him. *"You* think Batman's going to get me? Well, I think poison ivy is going to get you!"

Harley snapped her fingers and a vine reached a leafy shoot toward Robin. He recognized the leaves of the plant Poison Ivy was named for. Wherever it touched him, it would leave an itchy, blistering rash.

"Hey!" Robin shouted as the vine began to twine up his leg. "Stop! Get it off of me!"

***

Batman was crouched near a skylight in the middle of the roof when he heard Robin's panicked shout. Forgetting caution, he slapped on his rebreather mask and hooked his grapnel onto the edge of the skylight. Holding onto its cord, he kicked down on the skylight with the heel of his boot. *SMASH!*

The glass shattered, sending shards raining onto the plants below. The Dark Knight dropped through the opening and hung suspended as he quickly scanned the interior.

A forest of mostly gigantic, mutant plants were directly below Batman. Robin was tied to a stake at the far end of the room. Harley Quinn was standing near him, glaring up at the Caped Crusader.

"That's Batman!" she shouted to the plants. "Get him!"

A massive fern reached up with a frond as thick as a tentacle. It grabbed Batman by the leg and tugged.

Like an octopus, Batman thought. He pulled an explosive Batarang from his Utility Belt and hurled it into the fern.

BA-BOOM!

It blew apart the tentacle and the huge plant shrank away. Batman landed lightly in an open area between the foliage.

Batman had seen the vine that was beginning to twine around Robin. It looked too small to be life threatening, but he didn't want to take that chance. He raced down the aisle toward the Boy Wonder and Harley Quinn.

***

Harley scowled at Batman. This was so unfair! She had only cared for Red's plants for a few days and, because of Batman, her giant fern was damaged. It was *always* Batman who messed up her plans and made her life miserable. Well she had had enough!

Harley snatched her mallet and flipped down the aisle. She struck Batman in the chest with her mallet, knocking him backward into a monster vine. Instantly, it wrapped its tendrils around him, holding him so tight he couldn't reach his Utility Belt.

To Harley's surprise, the Harley Holly loped past her, slashing at Batman with its sharp leaves. Batman's uniform protected his body while the rebreather mask kept him from breathing in toxin as its berries burst. Still the little plant didn't give up.

"Holly's too small to really damage you," she told Batman. "But I know a plant that's big and mean, and very, very hungry!"

Behind her, the monstrous Venus flytrap loomed, its meat-eating blossom straining forward on its slender stalk. Its jaws opened wide. Its fangs glistened.

"All you had to do was free Red and my Puddin', but *nooooo!*" Harley said. "You had to play the hero! So now you and Robin are *both* gonna feed the plants!"

"I don't think so," Batman said. He rolled slightly, shifting his angle, and the little holly plant's dagger-sharp leaves sliced through the tendrils that bound his left arm. *SNICK! SNIP!* For an instant, it was free!

Batman snatched a Batarang from his Utility Belt and threw it. It hit Harley in the stomach, knocking her backward into the open maw of the Venus flytrap.

"Batman! Help!" Harley shouted, as the monster jaws closed around her with a *SNAP!*

But Batman could do nothing. The creeper vine had once again wrapped him in its tendrils so tightly that he couldn't move.

***

While Batman had confronted Harley, Robin had been tugging madly at his ropes, distracted by the threatening ivy plant that brushed against his cheek. He had missed most of their fight so he was surprised when he heard Harley's cry for help.

The Boy Wonder looked up as the last knot gave way. He realized both Harley and Batman were in trouble.

Robin pulled away from the stake and the clinging poison ivy plant. He had learned earlier that the plants were afraid of fire, and so he knew just what to do.

Robin rushed toward Batman and Harley, pulling a flash grenade from his Utility Belt. He hurled it at the creeper vine that held Batman captive.

The grenade exploded, releasing a quick burst of heat and light. The creeper shrank away, and Batman was free!

"Help me!" Harley shouted. Her head, one arm, and part of one leg stuck out of the monster plant's maw, but the rest of her had disappeared.

Robin hurled Glue Globules at any attacking plants, sticking their leaves and stems together, as Batman pulled a laser from his Utility Belt. A thin beam of light shot from it — *ZAP!* — slicing through the stem of the Venus flytrap. Its monstrous head slammed onto the floor with Harley inside.

While Robin kept the other plants at bay, Batman pulled her free. Harley was covered in sticky, stinking plant goo, but she wasn't hurt. Still, it had been a close call, and she knew it.

"Why didn't you just free my friends?" Harley wailed as Batman snapped handcuffs around her wrists. "I was lonely. I wanted you to know how it feels to lose someone. I just wanted to be with the people I love best."

Batman smiled grimly. "Think about it this way," he said as Robin led Harley from the warehouse. "You'll soon be with them, all together, in Arkham Asylum."

"That's true," Harley said, cheering up. "And all together, we can think of a way to escape! We have a lot of experience getting out of Arkham."

As police cars roared toward the greenhouse, sirens wailing, Harley had an awful thought. "Until we escape, you'll water Red's plants, right? And feed my pets? I have two hyenas, Giggles and Crackers. They're very sweet."

"Where are they?" the Dark Knight asked.

"They're in the Joker's secret hideout," Harley replied cheerfully. "I'll give you the address."

Behind her back, Robin rolled his eyes. He figured the Gotham Zoo would take good care of Harley's pets. But the Joker would be angry that she had revealed the location of his hideout.

Harley loved the Joker, but she clearly didn't understand him.

The sun was peeking over the horizon as the police van drove away with Harley Quinn inside. Batman looked after her thoughtfully. "She may be insane, but she's loyal to her friends."

"Like you!" Robin hesitated. "You weren't worried about me, were you?"

"I knew you could escape." Batman smiled. "You've been practicing. Which worked out very well, since you used that skill to free me."

Together, Batman and Robin fired their grapnels at the roof.

"It's good to have Harley back in Arkham," Robin said as the cords pulled them upward.

Batman and Robin climbed into the Batplane. "Let's go home," Batman said. "I understand *Veggie Wars* is waiting."

Robin scratched at the itchy blisters rising on his cheek. "I think I'll start a different video game," he muttered. "Right now, I'm sick of fighting plants."

HARLEY QUINN

REAL NAME: Dr. Harleen Quinzel

OCCUPATION: Psychiatrist, Professional Criminal

BASE: Gotham City

HEIGHT: 5 feet 7 inches

WEIGHT: 135 pounds

EYES: Blue

HAIR: Blond

Dr. Harleen Quinzel was once a successful psychiatrist at Gotham City's Arkham Asylum. But when she met the Joker, everything changed. When the Joker told Harley the heartbreaking, yet fake, story of his troubled childhood, her heart was won over. Harley fell in love with the Joker and soon helped him escape. She now clowns around Gotham City as Harley Quinn, the Joker's girlfriend and partner in crime.

- Poison Ivy is one of Harley's best friends. When the Clown Prince of Crime is in lockup, Harley and Ivy often team up. Their crazy capers around Gotham City usually provide the Dynamic Duo with a double dose of trouble.

- Harley's skills as a gymnast and acrobat make her a formidable fighter. She is also immune to many chemicals and diseases, thanks to a toxin antidote provided by Poison Ivy. This antidote also gives Harley enhanced strength and stamina.

- Harley's main weapon of choice is an oversized, wooden mallet. Despite its immense size, she can swing it with ease to fight off any foe. Harley also carries a cork gun from time to time. When fired, the cork often releases knockout gas or ropes to tie up her opponents.

BIOGRAPHIES

Louise Simonson enjoys writing about monsters, science fiction, fantasy characters, and super heroes. She has authored the award-winning Power Pack series, several best-selling X-Men titles, the Web of Spider-Man series for Marvel Comics, and the Superman: Man of Steel series for DC Comics. She has also written many books for kids. Louise is married to comic artist and writer Walter Simonson and lives in the suburbs of New York City.

Luciano Vecchio was born in 1982 and currently lives in Buenos Aires, Argentina. With experience in illustration, animation, and comics, his works have been published in the US, Spain, UK, France, and Argentina. His credits include *Ben 10* (DC Comics), *Cruel Thing* (Norma), *Unseen Tribe* (Zuda Comics), and *Sentinels* (Drumfish Productions).

GLOSSARY

artifact (AR-tuh-fact)—an object used in the past that was made by people

bulletin (BUL-uh-tuhn)—a short, important news report on TV or the radio

gargoyle (GAR-goil)—a stone head or figure carved below the roof of old buildings such as churches and museums

hyena (hye-EE-na)—a large dog-like animal that lives in Africa and Asia

immune (ih-MYOON)—not affected by something

infrared (in-fruh-RED)—a type of light that is invisible to human eyes

mallet (MAL-it)—a hammer with a short handle and a heavy wooden head

mutant (MYOOT-uhnt)—a living thing that has developed different characteristics than its parents had

spore (SPOR)—a plant cell produced by plants that do not flower, such as fungi, mosses, and ferns

tentacle (TEN-tuh-kuhl)—a long, flexible limb, similar to a leg or an arm, used for moving, feeling, and grabbing

toxin (TOK-sin)—a poisonous substance produced by a living thing

DISCUSSION QUESTIONS

1. Throughout the story, the perspective switches between the Dynamic Duo and Harley Quinn. Why does the author do this? How does seeing Harley's side of the story make you feel about her?

2. Poison Ivy's plants sometimes help Harley, but other times they attack her. Whose side are they on? Why do you think they behave the way they do?

3. Robin really wants to play his new video game but keeps getting interrupted by super-villain plots. Discuss a time when you really wanted to do an activity, but something else kept getting in the way. Explain how you felt.

WRITING PROMPTS

1. After Batman and Robin capture Poison Ivy, Harley goes to Ivy's secret greenhouse lab to water her plants. Write about a time you took care of a friend's pets or plants. Describe what went right and what went wrong.

2. Poison Ivy uses plants to commit crimes. Create a super hero who uses plants to conquer crime instead. Write a short story featuring your new super hero, then draw a picture of him or her.

3. At the end of the story, Batman and Robin capture Harley and send her to Arkham Asylum. Continue her story. Write about what happens when Harley gets there and reconnects with the Joker and Poison Ivy.